ARCADIA SCHOOL E. M. C.

 W9-DHL-262

THE BEAR'S TOOTHACHE

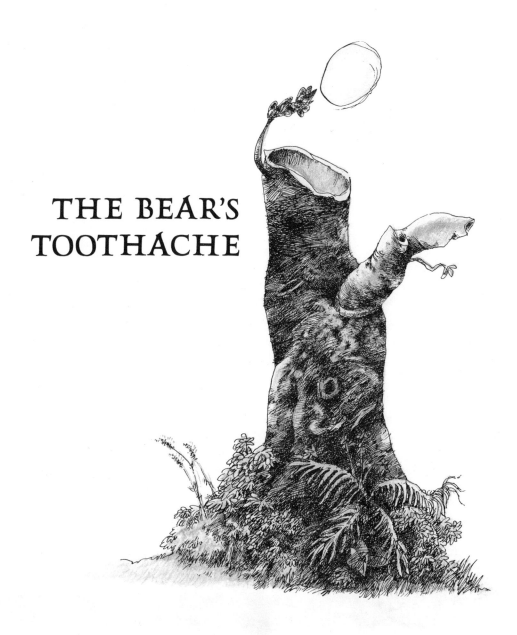

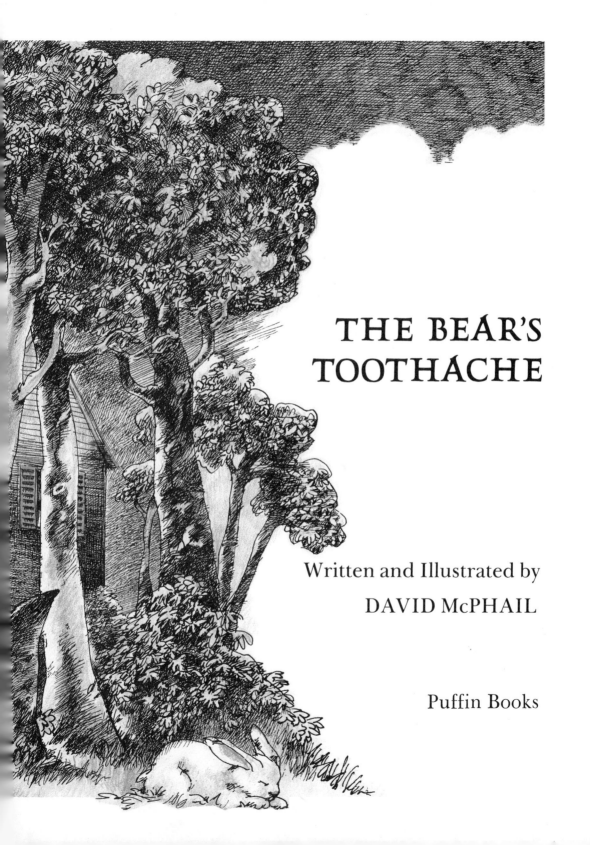

THE BEAR'S TOOTHACHE

Written and Illustrated by

DAVID McPHAIL

Puffin Books

Penguin Books Ltd, Harmondsworth, Middlesex, England
Penguin Books, 40 West 23rd Street, New York, NY 10010
Penguin Books Australia Ltd, Ringwood, Victoria, Australia
Penguin Books Canada Limited, 2801 John Street, Markham, Ontario, Canada L3R 1B4
Penguin Books (N.Z.) Ltd, 182-190 Wairau Road, Auckland 10, New Zealand .

First published by Little, Brown and Company, 1972
Reprinted by arrangement with Little, Brown and Company
in association with the Atlantic Monthly Press
Published in Puffin Books 1978
Reprinted 1980, 1981, 1983, 1984

Copyright © David McPhail, 1972
All rights reserved

Library of Congress Cataloging in Publication Data
McPhail, David M.   The bear's toothache.
Summary: When he discovers a bear with a toothache
outside his window, a little boy tries to think of ways
of removing the tooth.
I. Title.
PZ7.M2427Be   1978   [E]   77-12312
ISBN 0-14-050263-7

Printed in the United States of America by
Rae Publishing Co., Inc., Cedar Grove, New Jersey
Set in Baskerville

Except in the United States of America, this book is sold subject
to the condition that it shall not, by way of trade or otherwise,
be lent, re-sold, hired out, or otherwise circulated without
the publisher's prior consent in any form of binding or
cover other than that in which it is published and without a
similar condition including this condition being imposed on
the subsequent purchaser

For my son, Tristian
for Dr. Katherine Leland
for Dr. Arthur Bernstein
and
for Toughie the Bear

THE BEAR'S TOOTHACHE

One night I heard something
outside my window.

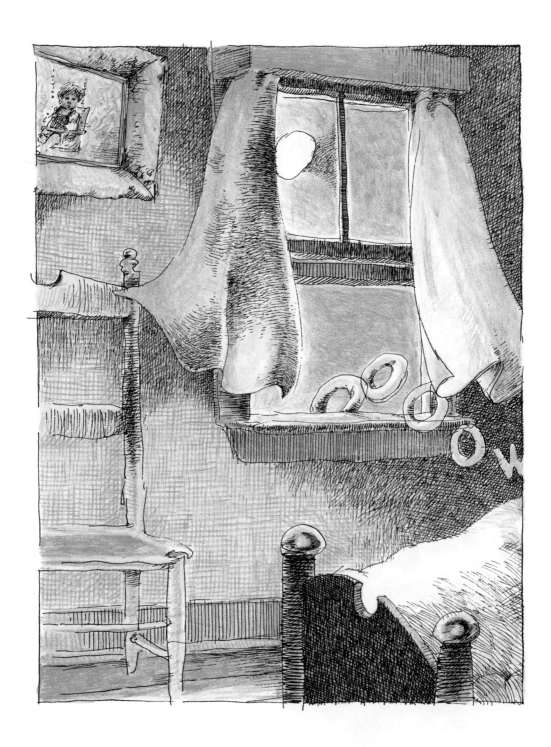

It was a bear

with a toothache.

I invited him in

and examined his teeth.

When I found the one that ached,
I tried to pull it out.

It wouldn't budge.

"Maybe some steak will loosen it
a little," said the bear.
So we went down to the kitchen,
where the bear chewed on some steak
and anything else he could find.

Pretty soon the food was all gone,
but the tooth was no looser than before.

When we got back to my room,
I tried to hit the tooth with my pillow.

But the bear ducked,
and I hit the lamp instead
and knocked it to the floor.
Crash!

The noise woke my father,
who got up and came to my room.

"What happened to the lamp?" he asked.

"It fell on the floor," I answered.

"Oh," he said, and he went back to bed.

Then I had a good idea.

I tied one end of my cowboy rope
to the bear's tooth

and tied the other end to the bedpost.

Then the bear stood on the windowsill

and jumped.

And just as he hit the ground,

the tooth popped out!

The bear was so happy that
he gave me the tooth

to put under my pillow.